PANTHER

Martin Booth was born in England but lived in Hong Kong from 1950 to 1964, where he was educated. As well as writing novels, he is a dedicated conservationist and has written television wildlife documentaries and a book on the ecology of African rhinos. He is also experienced in tracking big game.

Some other books by Martin Booth

MUSIC ON THE BAMBOO RADIO
WAR DOG

SURFERS

PANTHER

Martin Booth

Illustrated by
Sam Hadley

PUFFIN BOOKS

For Kate Lauder

PUFFIN BOOKS

Published by the Penguin Group
Penguin Books Ltd, 27 Wrights Lane, London W8 5TZ, England
Penguin Putnam Inc., 375 Hudson Street, New York, New York 10014, USA
Penguin Books Australia Ltd, Ringwood, Victoria, Australia
Penguin Books Canada Ltd, 10 Alcorn Avenue, Toronto, Ontario, Canada M4V 3B2
Penguin Books (NZ) Ltd, Private Bag 102902, NSMC, Auckland, New Zealand

Penguin Books Ltd, Registered Offices: Harmondsworth, Middlesex, England

First published 1999
5 7 9 10 8 6 4

Text copyright © Martin Booth, 1999
Illustrations copyright © Sam Hadley, 1999
All rights reserved

The moral right of the author and illustrator has been asserted

Set in Bembo

Made and printed in England by Clays Ltd, St Ives plc

British Library Cataloguing in Publication Data
A CIP catalogue record for this book is available from the British Library

ISBN 0–140–38978–4

Contents

Chapter One
The Three Hs

HOW LONG PATI had been asleep, she
could not tell. When she woke, it was
with a start.

She listened hard, holding her breath.
Something was scratching about outside
the caravan. It was not loud, but insistent,
frantic. She could only just hear it over

her father's gentle, wheezing snore. It was joined by a sort of purring.

Very slowly, so as not to make the caravan creak, Pati reached over and gradually slid the curtain along on its rail.

Outside, the moonlight was bright. In the caravan's shadow was a small plastic dustbin. She pressed her cheek to the cold glass. Something black was moving around the bin. The purring was louder.

In Pati's mind, a series of ordered images appeared. It was as if she were looking round her bedroom at home, at her posters of the snarling tiger, the jaguar crouched by a stream in the Amazonian jungle, the pride of lions with blood-stained muzzles tearing a zebra carcass, the Rocky Mountain cougar feasting on a deer. Only the leopard asleep in the fork of a tree was not menacing. The cheetah behind the door was in full flight after a baby gazelle: in the poster over the stereo, it had it by the throat.

As she thought of her posters, Pati remembered one initial fact: at times, even big cats scavenge for food.

Suddenly, as if it sensed her watching, the animal by the dustbin froze. The purring immediately stopped. Every nerve in Pati's body was as taut as the strings of a violin bow. For a moment, all was still. Then, with a shambling movement, the creature raced into the moonlight and vanished into the hedge. For a brief moment, Pati saw a black-and-white striped head.

Disappointed, she rolled back on her bunk but did not fall asleep immediately. Reaching under her pillow, she pulled out her pen torch and, keeping it under the duvet so as not to wake her parents, switched it on. From inside the book she was reading, wedged down the side of the thin mattress, she took out her most recent newspaper cutting and read the headline:

DEVON 'PANTHER' SLAUGHTERS SIX LAMBS
Sheep Farmers Irate at Big Cat Threat

I'll bet it was dogs, she thought. Sheep worriers. No big cat would kill six lambs for sheer fun. It would only kill one, to eat. She scanned the article. There was no mention of any of the lambs being eaten, only mutilated.

By the time Pati next woke, the sun was up. It was warm upon her skin as she stepped out of the caravan. Simon was sitting on a folding chair in front of his parents' caravan parked nearby, reading a wildlife magazine.

"Hi, Si!" Pati greeted him.

Simon looked up. "Hi, Pats. You hear anything during the night?"

"It was only a badger," Pati replied sadly, adding, "Have they gone?"

"Long ago," Simon answered briefly.

"Why do our fathers *do* it?" Pati wondered aloud. "Same weekend, every year. I mean, where's the enjoyment in trout fishing?"

"I suppose," Simon said, "if we worked all day at a desk in Mercantile Marine Management Consultants, we'd do something like fishing . . ."

"Not me!" Pati declared, sitting on the bench by the picnic table. "Besides, I'm not going to be a computer disk jockey."

Pati knew what she wanted to be – a naturalist making television wildlife documentaries. Simon wanted to be a gamekeeper or, in his wildest dreams, a game warden in Africa.

"That's my target animal this weekend," Simon declared, holding the magazine open at a two-page spread of a stag with a full set of antlers.

"Nice one," Pati said absent-mindedly. Simon knew what she was thinking and asked, "Do you really believe there's a big cat living on the moors in the West Country?"

"Could be," said Pati. "People've taken photos — even videos — of it."

"People've taken photos of the Loch Ness Monster and Bigfoot," Simon remarked. "Doesn't mean they exist. A bit of driftwood bobbing on the water, a man in a monkey suit." He made a face, scratched his armpit and grunted. "None of the pictures've been clear."

"No," Pati said thoughtfully, "but they're all possible. Think, Si! Only a few years ago, they found a new species of deer in Vietnam. Totally unknown to science."

"Vietnam's got jungles, mountains, swamps," Simon replied sharply. "This is England. Towns, villages, fields, motorways."

Pati nodded. "True. You'd think at least one would be found run over. Foxes and badgers are hit by cars . . ."

"If it was run over, that would be the end of it," Simon stated.

Pati sighed and said, "Si, put your brain in gear."

"What do you mean?" Simon began, a little hurt.

"Put your brain round this," Pati said. "It's not *a* big cat."

"Well, if it's not a . . ." Then it dawned on him. "You mean there's a whole colony of them!"

"Colony!" snorted Pati mockingly. "They're not ants."

"What are you two up to today?"

Simon's mother asked, coming out of her caravan with plates of scrambled eggs. Pati's mother followed, carrying mugs of coffee.

"As if we need to ask!" Pati's mother exclaimed.

Simon's mother put the plates on the table.

"We're going to look for one of these," Simon announced, holding up his magazine.

"What is it?" his mother asked. "An antelope?"

Pati and Simon exchanged exasperated glances.

"It's a fallow deer," Simon said patiently. "Antelopes live in Africa."

"Be careful on the moor," Pati's mother warned them. However, she wasn't too worried about them going off. Pati knew what she was doing and Simon, though he was younger, was no fool.

"Back by seven," Simon's mother went on. "No later. Supper's at half past. If you're not back by dark, you know what'll happen?"

"Yes, Mum," Simon replied. "We know. *The Three Hs.* Help, Helicopters and Hospitals."

Chapter Two
Wisht Hounds

PATI PICKED UP her rucksack and, before zipping it shut, checked her most important possession. It had been her present for her fourteenth birthday, a few months ago. Pushing her hand inside the zip, her fingers touched the cool body of her compact Canon camera.

11

This was no point-'n'-shoot family snappy camera. This was what her father called Serious Kit. Dull gold in colour, the camera was a Z135 model with a 1:3.6 to 8.9 zoom lens, automatic DX code film loading, a simplified picture mode selector mechanism with sport, night, portrait and macro settings and an automatic flash-off facility. It might not have been a single-lens reflex camera such as wildlife photographers used, but it was the next best thing to it.

Besides the Canon, she had a spare film, three energy-rich Mars bars – she remembered the old saying, *chocolate chivvies you up, sandwiches slow you down* – an apple, a battered ex-army aluminium canteen of water, painted brown, and a dark green, mottled forage cap. If they wanted to stalk animals, her shoulder-length blonde hair had to be covered.

Simon carried a similar rucksack only instead of Mars bars, he had two blocks of Cadbury's Fruit'n'Nut. Instead of a camera, he carried his best present from the previous Christmas: a pair of Chinon 10 x 50 binoculars.

It was nine o'clock when they set off, crossing the river by a sturdy plank bridge near a copse of beech trees. They climbed a low rise and paused. Ahead of them, the moors spread out like a rolling carpet. The horizon was spiked here and there by jagged stone outcrops and tors, sharp peaks of barren rock.

The sun was high and warm, the sky dotted with fair weather cumulus clouds. The only sign of the modern world was a thin vapour trail scrawled across the sky by a transatlantic jumbo jet.

At first, neither Pati nor Simon saw any animals at all. This did not concern them. It was not that there were none. They knew the moors were alive with creatures. It was simply that their eyes were not yet tuned in to seeing them.

Gradually, however, they started to notice animals. What appeared to be grey granite boulders in the distance were recognized to be sheep, not rocks. A patch of dense bush moved and turned out to be a wild pony. A clump of immobile grass evolved into a very mobile rabbit.

By one o'clock, in addition to the common animals living on the moor, they had spied two hares and a weasel hunting mice. Also, much to Pati's delight for she had never seen one before, they spotted a common lizard basking on a smooth rock.

Simon had seen the reptile first from some way off. Pati, with infinite patience, had then got close enough to photograph it. At least, she hoped she had. The minute the camera shutter clicked, the lizard was gone, flicking itself into a crack in the rock.

They climbed a high tor to have a rest. There, they lazed in the sun like the lizard and ate their chocolate. It was now soft and sticky in their warm rucksacks and they had to suck it off their fingers. When they opened their canteens, the water was as warm as tea.

They lay side by side on their

stomachs on a flat rock and watched the pattern of the clouds skimming over the moors below. The heather and scrub changed colour under the shadows and glaring sunlight.

Simon levelled his binoculars at a circle of boulders half a mile away on a sloping hillside. In the ring, two sheep were grazing the short grass.

"Funny to think Bronze Age people were living here six thousand years ago," Simon remarked. "I wonder what those stone circles were for."

"Some are hut circles, some are like miniature Stonehenges," Pati replied. A cloud overhead moved away on a stiff breeze. She squinted her eyes in the sudden glare. "They're where they worshipped the sun."

"If they all lived here," Simon continued, scanning his binoculars across the moor, "they must have all died here. So, under the moors —" his voice took on a ghostly tone — "there must be thousands and thousands of dead people in ancient graves. Buried with bronze axes and helmets and shields and gold jewellery."

"So," Pati asked, "you going to change your mind?"

"Change my mind?"

"Dump biology for archaeology. Give up natural history for ancient history," Pati said. "Sell your binocs and buy a spade."

"No," Simon answered. "But you think. At night —" his voice turned spooky again — "those phantoms. Spirits

17

of dead warriors. Ghost–axes swinging in the moonlight."

Pati, not taking her eyes off the moor, said, "Never mind Bronze Age warriors, Si. You ever heard of the Wisht Hounds?"

"No," Simon replied bluntly, after a moment's thought. He had read all the books he could find on moorland wildlife but he did not recognize the name.

"In the middle of the moor," Pati began, "there's a place called Wistman's Wood. But this is no ordinary wood. The trees are stunted and gnarled and twisted like they're in pain. They grow out of boulders and rocks. Moss hangs from their branches and their bark's covered in lichen like the sores of lepers."

She paused, casting a sideways glance

at Simon. He had put his binoculars down and was looking straight at her. Pati knew he had a good imagination and was seeing the wood. With a bit of luck, she thought, he would have a nightmare that night.

"When it's a full moon," she continued, looking at the horizon with a faraway gaze, "the Wisht Hunt comes out of the wood. It's the Devil's own hunt, Satan's own pack of hounds. They have red eyes that burn like hot charcoal in the darkness. He rides a black horse with no head. The hounds howl as they hunt. If you see them, you'll die within a year. And if you don't see them, you'll hear them." She cupped her hands to her mouth and made a faint, eerie owl hoot.

Simon stared at her for a moment, then exclaimed, "That's all crap!"

Pati smiled and said brightly, "Probably. Old folks' tales. Just country legend. They say the hounds hunt unbaptized babies. That's a bit rich." She paused for effect then added, "Isn't it a full moon tomorrow night?"

"There's no such thing as Wisht Hounds!" Simon went on.

"I shouldn't think so," Pati agreed, "but then a lot of people don't think there's a big cat on the moors. So what kills the sheep?"

Simon put his binoculars to his eyes once more. Far off, over a rocky tor jutting into the sky, a large bird lazily rode the afternoon's thermal columns of hot air rising off the granite boulders.

"Buzzard," Simon declared. "It might be nesting over there. They sometimes nest on rocky ledges. Lays two to three eggs, white with brown markings. They hatch after thirty-six days. The buzzard's the nearest England has to an eagle."

It was all Pati could do to stop laughing. He was prattling and she knew she had hit the raw nerve of Simon's imagination. That nightmare, she thought, was a sure bet.

Chapter Three
Five Cautious Sheep

THEY LEFT THE tor about four o'clock, heading back to the campsite. The sun was still high and warm, the moors shimmering under a haze of heat. As they walked along a well-trodden path, they met a party of eight hikers coming towards them at a fair speed.

Each one was uniformly kitted out with a bright orange rucksack, wore heavy walking boots and carried a canary-yellow anorak rolled up on top of his pack. They walked in single file, not talking, striding out with a purpose.

Pati and Simon stepped aside to let them pass. Each hiker nodded his thanks but said nothing. The man taking up the rear wore a leather strap with a brass crown on it round his wrist. He was the only one who spoke.

"Keep goin', you slacking platoon of baboons!" he yelled at the men. Then, smiling to Pati and Simon, said, "Thank you. Third Brigade team. Training exercise. Only ten miles to go. Got to keep up the pace." And, with that, he jogged after them, his boots tapping out a steady rhythm on the dry soil.

When the soldiers had disappeared over a ridge, the sounds of the moor returned. High in the sky, unseen birds sang. Here and there, a wild pony grazed. A breeze hissed in the heather. Every now and then, a distant sheep bleated forlornly.

An hour later, they were about to descend into a wide shallow valley through which a little river wandered when Pati stopped and shaded her eyes against the sun. It was now lower in the sky. For at least a minute, she studied the valley before speaking.

"Si," she said quietly, "can you see anything down there?"

"Down where?"

"Down by the water. Where the path crosses the stream."

Simon raised his binoculars and focused on a clapper bridge, a huge and ancient slab of stone over the river, well over six metres long. Leading up to the stone were three or four steps cut into a boulder. Just to one side of the bridge stood a rowan tree, bent over by centuries of westerly wind.

"Got it," he said.

"Go right of the tree," Pati instructed. "About thirty metres. Some big rocks."

Obeying her command, Simon shifted his field of vision. A number of boulders came into view, the river tumbling between them over miniature rapids. He could see the sunlight sparkling off the surface.

"OK."

"What do you see?"

"Rocks, water . . ." said Simon.

Pati snatched the binoculars from Simon's hand, whipping the strap off his neck. It snagged on one of his ears.

"That hurt!" he exclaimed angrily.

"Shut up, Si!" Pati hissed, going down on her haunches, resting her elbows on her knees to steady the binoculars.

She quickly found the rowan tree, moved right, up a bit. There were the rocks and the water. Nothing moved in the shadows. Up a bit more. Left a bit, back towards the clapper bridge but on the far side of the stream. Five sheep. One sitting, four standing. All chewing absent-mindedly.

"What are you looking at?" Simon asked, squatting next to Pati.

"I'm not sure," she murmured, concentrating on the sheep. "Maybe nothing."

Suddenly, the sheep stopped chewing, all at the same time. They all looked in the same direction, towards the rocks. One bleated. The sitting sheep got clumsily to its feet.

Pati refocused on the rocks. Nothing. Back to the sheep. They were suddenly cautious. Their ears were up and their nostrils sniffed the breeze. Suddenly, they took flight, running over the heather and scrub like shaggy, animated bathmats.

Pati swung the binoculars to one side. There, walking slowly through a thick patch of heather, was a large, black animal. She could only see its back and the top of its head. Yet it moved in a certain way, with a kind of grace. A cat-like grace. She sucked her breath in.

"So," Simon asked, a bit peeved at Pati hogging his binoculars, "what is it? Do I get a look?"

Pati made no effort to return the binoculars. She could not bring herself to lower them from her eyes.

"It's a . . ." She paused.

"It's a what?" Simon asked impatiently.

She could not believe it. She wanted to believe it but her mind filled with self-doubt. Maybe, like all those photographers and video camera owners before her, she was being taken in by a trick of the light. Maybe it was nothing more than a shadow, a darker-than-usual fox, a dog — a black Labrador — on the loose.

"It's . . ." Pati answered in a half-whisper. "It's a panther. A black panther."

Chapter Four
A Signature in the Mud

SIMON GRABBED THE binoculars from
Pati's hands.

"Let me have a look," he demanded,
not believing her.

Yet just at the very moment he
snatched them, Pati saw the animal
disappear into a dip in the ground.

30

"I can't see anything," Simon said, sweeping the moor to find the creature.

"It's gone," Pati said.

"Gone!" Simon snorted. "Wisht Hounds to you!"

Pati stood up slowly. Her mind was going over the clues that told her it was a big cat.

"No," she said, her confidence growing. "It was a panther. The ears were round, not pointed like a dog's. I saw its shoulders moving. Like a cat's. And its back —"

"I thought panthers were nocturnal. It's —" Simon looked at his watch — "only a quarter to six."

Pati considered this truth then said, "They are seen by daylight. It was probably drinking after hiding up all day, before setting out to hunt."

31

"Did you see its tail?" Simon inquired, his voice touched with sarcasm. "All brown and bushy and labelled *Property of Basil Brush*?"

"I know a fox when I see one," Pati retorted indignantly, "and that wasn't one. And I'll prove it."

Not waiting for Simon's answer or agreement, Pati set off running down the hill towards the river. At the clapper bridge, she stopped and waited for Simon to catch up.

"Right!" she said determinedly, catching her breath. "Now we'll see."

Following the river bank, they went towards the boulders upstream from the rowan tree. As they approached them, the musical tinkle of the water running over stones became louder.

"It was drinking," Pati stated. "Before the sheep were frightened."

Without a moment's hesitation, she clambered over the first boulder. Behind it the river was forced into a sharp curve by the rocks. On the outside of the bend, mud and silt had collected, forming a small muddy beach about a metre wide. The water was brown with the stain of peat off the moors. Pati leaned against a rock and looked down.

"There, Si!" she said with a deep satisfaction.

Simon joined her on the rock and looked down at the little mudbank. Impressed into the mud, so fresh that they had yet to fill with water, was a set of pug marks.

"It's just as good as if it had signed its name," Pati went on.

"Dog," Simon declared bluntly.

Pati slid down the boulder and landed on the mud. She bent down and studied the paw prints, her face within centimetres of them. She gently touched her finger into one of them, feeling round the rim.

When she straightened up, she wiped her hands on her jeans and declared, "Dogs have claws."

"So what?" Simon responded. "So do cats."

"Yes," agreed Pati, "but cats can retract them into sheaths in their toes. Dogs can't. Their claws are always out. These pug marks —" there was a triumphant glint in her eye — "have no claws."

Chapter Five
Trout and Raisins

AROUND THE OIL lamps set at each end of
the table was a glow of yellow light. It
turned the white wine in the bottle by
the salt and pepper shakers into the colour
of honey. A night breeze ruffled the edge
of the tablecloth. A near full moon had
just risen over the woods to the east,

35

across the river from the campsite, bathing the countryside in grey light.

Pati cast a look at Simon. He had his head buried in a book about game management. She smiled to herself. He was trying to keep his brain busy, concentrate on other things. It was, she thought, definitely a Wisht Hound night.

"Mind the bones," Simon's mother warned as she stepped back from the barbecue, holding a giant frying pan. "Trout's notorious for small bones."

Pati looked at her plate. Simon's mother was herself notorious for what she termed 'the art of creative cookery'. The trout smelled strangely of caramel. When Pati touched it with her knife, she discovered the skin was as crisp as dried leaves.

"This one fought like a demon!" Pati's father reported proudly, splitting his fish open with his knife. "Narrow river, fast flowing. Took him on a Greenwell's Glory — that's a dry fly," he added unnecessarily.

"Here we go again!" Pati's mother interrupted. "Dry flies and wet flies, buzzers and nymphs and lures. We've heard all about them, Derek. Now you've caught it, eat it."

Pati's father put a large flake of fish in his mouth, chewed it thoughtfully and swallowed it with a gulp of white wine. "Very interesting," he remarked. "What's in it, Liz?"

"Raisins," Simon's mother replied. "That's the stuffing. Raisins and a little rosemary. But first, it's marinated in brandy and brown sugar then shallow-fried in butter and chopped shallots."

After the meal was over, and the crockery washed and put away, the adults sat by the glimmer of the oil lamps under the caravan awning, playing bridge. Simon and Pati walked to the river's edge and sat on a flat rock overlooking the water. For some minutes, they did not speak.

"We must tell someone," Simon said finally. "The national park authority, English Nature, the police."

Pati remained silent, looking at the black water rushing past her feet. The moon was higher now, only the brightest stars visible through its glare.

"Maybe the National Farmers' Union should be told," Simon went on, "so farmers can protect their sheep and . . ."

"And what?" Pati cut in. "They'll say it's a danger to their stock, to wildlife, to humans. They'll call in marksmen or the army. Then the press will get the story. Hundreds of journalists running all over the moors, helicopters and TV crews buzzing about like wasps at a picnic. Thousands of sightseers, hunt supporters on motorbikes, Rambos with rifles out to bag themselves a big game trophy. And it'll go on and on and on until the last panther on the moor is hunted down, cornered and shot."

"So what do you say we do?" Simon asked.

Pati made no immediate reply. She picked up a pebble and tossed it into the river. The *plop!* of it hitting the surface was smothered by the general rush of the water.

"What we do," she said at last, turning to face Simon, "is keep our heads, keep our mouths shut and, tomorrow, stalk it."

"Stalk it!" Simon exclaimed, his eyes wide with amazement.

"Yes," Pati replied matter-of-factly. "We follow up its spoor. Observe it, study it, understand it. And, above all, photograph it. Right now, we've no proof it exists. I saw it. You didn't. If we went to the authorities, you know what they'd say."

"Two kids taking the mickey?" Simon suggested.

"Exactly. What we must do is get absolute proof the panther exists and know as much about it as we can. We must be able to prove the panther is no threat. If we can show that it eats rabbits and deer and not just sheep, and that it's no real danger, then when . . . if . . . it is ever discovered, we might stand a chance of having it conserved, not killed."

"And how do we stalk it?" Simon asked.

"Just like you do anything else," Pati said reassuringly. "Footprints, droppings, signs of a kill, a knowledge of the creature's habitat."

"We're not white hunters in the African bush," said Simon. "Stalking a fox or a roe deer's one thing. A panther's something else. I mean − what if it's a man-eater?"

Pati laughed. "You mean like a Wisht Hound?" she suggested.

"No! Be serious!" Simon demanded. "Think! How many people disappear every year? Hundreds. The police always assume they're murdered. Most of them are. But what if –"

"Life is one long *what if*!" Pati declared. "What if you got run over by a bus? What if your father lost his job? What if your mother was a serial killer? A chainsaw murderer? A mass poisoner?"

She thought briefly of the strange taste of the trout which still lingered in her mouth. Creative cookery could be used to disguise a multitude of poisons.

"You can't live your whole life wondering," Pati went on. "You've got to act. Make the *what if* into an *it is*. You've got a choice, Si. Get out and do something, or sit at home and watch the video."

She glanced at her digital watch. The moonlight was so bright, she could read it without pressing the illumination button.

"We've a long day tomorrow," she said, "and we have to start early. Big cats hunt at dawn and dusk. If we are to get a good sighting, we've got to be out and on the moor by dawn."

Simon rose to his feet. He had pins and needles in his right leg and rubbed it to get the nerves to stop tingling. Pati set the alarm on her watch. It chirped like a little electronic bird every time she pushed the button.

"What time?" Simon wanted to know, holding his own watch.

"Quarter-past four," Pati answered. "Even before our fathers get up. Then we can be well away and up on the moor by five-thirty."

When their watches were set, they walked slowly up to the caravans. They could soon hear the rowdy voices of their parents. The game of bridge was still in progress.

"Four spades!" Simon's father declared. He stared hard at his wife, who was his bridge partner, with a stern leave-it-at-that, don't-say-anything look.

"No bid," said Pati's father.

Simon's mother considered her hand of cards then replied, "Four no trumps!"

At that, Pati's parents fell about laughing and Simon's father pretended to lose his temper.

"Four no trumps!" he exploded in mock rage. "Four no trumps! Didn't you hear how I opened, you dozy old bat? I started with three clubs! That means shut up. Honestly, Liz, we're going down here."

He slapped his cards on the table and arranged them in suits. Then he wiped his hands on his T-shirt as if the cards had somehow dirtied his fingers. "Load of rubbish there! Hand like a foot! Anyone want another glass of wine while my wife tries to win a game in four no trumps with less than eighteen points in her delicate mitt?"

He picked up a bottle of wine from a bucket of ice by his chair. "At least we're only playing for matches, not money. And the way we're going, it'll be a long time before we're able to light the barbecue again."

Pati and Simon exchanged glances. They were both thinking the same thing. Parents on holiday were a totally different type of animal from parents at home.

Chapter Six
A Dusty Pug

ALONG THE HORIZON was the merest hint of daylight. Pati could not say at what moment it had appeared. One minute it was night and the next it was not. Very gradually, the darkness seemed to weaken. The air was chilled but fresh and clean when she sucked it in. She looked at her watch, not for the first time. It was twenty minutes to five.

Very slowly, the door of the other caravan opened and Simon stepped cautiously down to the ground. The chassis squeaked slightly as it was relieved of his weight.

"You're late," Pati hissed with annoyance.

Simon carefully closed the door, the catch making a single click as it caught.

"It's all right for you," he muttered under his breath. "Your parents sleep like the dead. My mother wakes if a mouse farts."

"Got everything?" Pati whispered. "We'll be out all day."

Simon checked his rucksack – water bottle, chocolate, a small first-aid kit, a perspex orienteering compass, a penknife with a serrated blade and his binoculars. His check completed, he nodded and murmured, "You?"

Pati had already made sure she had all she needed. She carried the same as Simon except that, as well as chocolate, she had high energy glucose tablets and, in place of the binoculars, she had her camera and two rolls of spare film. In addition, she had included her halogen-bulbed Mag-Lite torch and a red plastic whistle, to blow if they were trapped somewhere out of sight of rescuers.

It was not that Pati intended to let herself get into a situation where rescue was needed. The last thing she wanted was Simon's mother's Three Hs turning up and ruining her hunt.

As they headed out over the moor, the daylight grew stronger. Vague shadows turned into rocks and clumps of heather. The sky was clear, almost empty of clouds. There was absolutely no wind. The only sound was that of their boots on the pathway or their jeans brushing against a bush or clump of long grass. At a quarter to six, when the sun was well up, they reached the clapper bridge.

By the bridge, it was dusty where hikers' boots had marched over the dry soil. Pati stopped and studied the dust. Imprinted into it was a single, solitary pug mark.

"There!" she said with quiet satisfaction. "It uses the clapper bridge. I knew it would. Most big cats – except tigers – don't really like water and will use a bridge if there is one." She studied the pug mark closely. "It went over this bridge about four hours ago."

"How can you tell that!" Simon exclaimed.

"Look," Pati said and, next to the pug mark, she pressed her hand into the dust. "See how the dust in the panther's paw mark is sort of flat. Now, look at the dust in my hand print. The dust in the middle is sort of fluffy and the edges are sharp. The pug mark edges are blunt. They've started to wear away with time."

She stood up and rubbed out the two marks with her hiking boot.

"Best to cover all our tracks," she declared.

They stepped up on to the slab of stone and crossed the river. On the far side, the ground was stony and they couldn't see any trail at all.

"How did you know about that dust business?" Simon asked.

"I read it," Pati answered simply, "in a book about ivory hunters in Kenya. Then I tried it out. Watched what happened to our moggie's paw marks after he walked through our garden. Last summer, when it was dry and we weren't allowed to use the hosepipe."

They walked up to the top of a ridge and stopped to sit on a boulder. The sun was bright, but the morning air still carried a sharp nip in it. It would be another hour before it started to warm up.

For fifteen minutes Pati studied every part of the moor before them while

Simon did the same with his binoculars. He swept from left to right then back again, the angle of the binoculars slightly lower with every sweep.

"Nothing!" he remarked at length.

"There's something there," Pati said, "it's just that we haven't seen it yet."

"Where do you think the panther's gone?" Simon wondered.

"It all depends," Pati replied. "If it's made a kill, it might lie up near it, but otherwise it will have gone into hiding for the day. Either —" she pointed to a line of woodland on the horizon two miles away across the moor — "it's headed for the trees or it's going to spend the day in the rocks of a tor."

"That's a bit in the open," said Simon.

"But safe," Pati went on. "Fewer

people on the tors. And that is a natural hiding place. Leopards often live on *kopjes* – they're rocky outcrops on the African veld – that's what the grass plains are called."

"I know what the veld is," Simon complained peevishly. "I do read too, you know. Anyway," he continued, "this is not a leopard. It's a panther. That's what all the newspaper reports say. And panthers live in South America, leopards live in Africa and India . . ."

"Well, actually," Pati said, "some people think this isn't a South American animal at all. And, anyway, black panthers are really melanic leopards."

Pati paused. She was always ready to score a point against Simon.

For a moment, Simon said nothing

then his curiosity got the better of him and he asked, "What's melanic?"

"A hybrid. One that's gone black," she said smugly, winning the point. "Anyway," she went on, "even panthers will live in rocky areas. That's where you find them in the Andes. They're –"

"Mountains in South America," Simon stopped her. "I'm not that dense."

For a while, they did not speak again, but watched the moor. As the sun climbed higher, the animals began to go about their day.

The sheep, that had bunched together during the night, started to saunter apart, grazing here and there. The moorland ponies slowly made their way to the nearest water to drink. Buzzards started to appear, riding the new thermal columns of air rising from the warming rocks. Larks hovered invisibly in the sky, singing.

In the far distance, Simon caught sight of a deer through his binoculars. It had a fine spread of antlers and its rump was marked with cream spots. It had to be a fallow stag.

"Ha!" he said with quiet satisfaction. "I've got my target animal."

Pati didn't shift her eyes from the moor as she replied, "Good. Now we get mine."

Chapter Seven
Where There's a Crow

FROM THE RIDGE, they walked across a wide valley and then went around the edge of a peat bog. Even so, they were too close. No sooner had their boots started to squelch than Simon's right foot went in up to the ankle.

57

"I'm stuck!" he exclaimed with annoyance.

Pati, who was standing upon firmer ground, looked at his foot. As he spoke, it went in another centimetre. His left boot was already in up to the lower lace holes.

"Don't take a step," Pati ordered Simon. Her voice was calm so as not to panic him, but, at the same time, as insistent as a strict teacher. "Lift your left foot and —" she looked around — "fall on to that hump."

For a moment, Simon stood quite still. He suddenly realized the danger he was in. He felt his face pale and his breath quicken. Turning, he obeyed Pati's command and let himself fall on to a large clump of grass and spiky sedge.

"That's spread your weight," Pati said. "Now you'll be OK."

She grabbed him by the wrists and pulled. There was a slurping sound as his foot came free. A faint smell of dead leaves and methane marsh gas drifted past them on the breeze.

Simon and Pati went back the way they had come. They trod gingerly, not too hastily. Once on solid ground again, they exchanged glances.

"You think it is?" Simon wondered aloud.

Pati picked up a large stone the size of a grapefruit and, tucking it into her shoulder, pitched it forward like a shot-putter. It flopped on to the peat with a wet thump. They watched. In less than a minute, the stone had disappeared.

"Quagmire," Pati half whispered, a shiver running up her spine. Once you were trapped in that, she thought, you had no future but to drown in soggy, cloying peat.

"Thanks, Pats," Simon said meekly.

"A friend in need's always better than the Three Hs," she replied and she gave him a grin.

When they arrived on the next ridge, they stopped to study the land beyond it. By now the sun was hot. Pati took off her waterproof jacket and folded it into her rucksack.

At first, they did not see it. Then, quite suddenly, Pati realized what she was looking at. There was one spot on the moor, about 800 metres away, to which a number of crows were heading.

"We've got it!" she exclaimed. "You know what that means?" She did not wait for Simon's reply. "Crows are to England what vultures are to Africa. Where there's a crow, there's carrion. And carrion means a kill."

"It might not be a panther kill," Simon remarked. "It could be a dead fox or a dead rabbit."

"It's big," Pati replied. "Too many crows for a rabbit. It's a sheep."

"It could be a pony," Simon said.

Pati gave him a withering look. She was sure this was a sheep and longed for it to be a panther kill. A panther was not big enough to bring down a pony. It could drop a foal, but even that was not too likely. Ponies were fleet of foot and a panther was no cheetah. It could not run fast over any real distance.

"Ponies and sheep die of old age," Simon added.

"Shut up, Si!" Pati snapped, tugging her rucksack over her shoulder. "You are an MLG."

With that, she set off at a brisk pace through the heather and scrub, ignoring any paths and making directly for the conference of crows.

"What's an MLG?" Simon called, running to catch up with her and trying to work out what the initials stood for.

"A Miserable Little Git," Pati told him.

There was no need to approach with caution. If the crows were there, the panther would not be. Like vultures, they would not approach if the big cat was on the kill, but would perch on nearby rocks, waiting their turn at the feast.

As they came closer, a flurry of crows took to the air, cawing with annoyance at being driven from their meal. Just as Pati predicted, it was a sheep. The carcass, which was lying on its right side, was half hidden under a big rock.

"It's a kill," she declared with a certain pride. "See how the panther's tried to tuck it out of sight of the crows? Big cats do that. Leopards and panthers also take their kills into trees to stop scavengers."

"Not many trees round here," said Simon.

"Precisely, Si," Pati replied. "Now help me pull it out."

"Won't that disturb it?" Simon said. "If you disturb a kill . . ."

"The panther won't return to this kill," Pati announced. "For a start, it'll smell that humans have been here and that will alarm it. Second, if it was going to return, it would be lying up near by."

"How do you know it isn't?" Simon asked with a touch of anxiety, looking at the surrounding rocks and boulders. Now that he thought about it, the panther could be hiding in any number of places within a hundred-metre radius of where they stood.

"If it was," Pati answered, "the crows would be more cautious. You don't need to worry, Si."

Grabbing the dead sheep by its hind legs, they tugged it into the open. At once Pati knelt down to work out how the creature had died.

"Look, Si," she said excitedly. "Here, on the sheep's back, there are claw marks and here –" she poked her finger on to a bald patch where the fleece was missing – "is where the claws pulled a big tuft of wool out. Now look at its neck."

The sheep's throat bore deep teeth marks.

"It's a classic panther kill!" Pati exclaimed with delight. "The panther stalked the sheep. At the last minute, as it started to leap, the sheep took fright. It ran. The panther ran after it, jumped on its back to bring it down, gripped it by the throat and throttled it to death."

The front left shoulder of the sheep

had been eaten, along with a part of the belly. Blood was matted in the fleece, but generally there was not as much blood as Simon had expected. He had thought they would find a mess of meat, but in fact the sheep was still more or less intact. The crows had had a go at the rump but they had not found the carcass all that long ago.

"Let's roll it over," Pati said.

"Why?" Simon wanted to know. After all, a dead sheep was a dead sheep.

Pati did not reply. She had her reasons.

Together, they manhandled the carcass, turning it on to its left side. As it went over, the grey-green intestines fell out and started to unravel like a string of sickly sausages. A terrible stench drifted on the air. Simon felt the bile rise in his throat and swallowed hard, fighting against throwing up.

When he glanced at Pati, it seemed as if she was not in the least affected by it. Without flinching for one second, she thrust her hand deep into the sheep's body cavity.

"What the hell are you doing?" Simon exclaimed with disgust.

Pati withdrew her arm. It was smeared with half-congealed blood, almost as far up as her elbow.

"It's still fairly warm," she announced. "I'd say this sheep was killed less than two hours ago." She tore a handful of grass free and started to wipe the blood off her skin. "If you'd got up on time, Si, we might have seen the panther make this kill."

"So what do we do now?" Simon asked, stepping back out of range of the stink of the spilled guts.

For a moment, Pati considered the options. Clearly, the panther was not lying up near its kill. The crows told her that much. On the other hand, it could not be too far away. It had made its kill since dawn and must have stayed with it well after sun-up to eat as much as it had.

It was, she thought, not very likely that it had returned to the cover of the distant woodland which was at least three miles away. No panther would risk such a long journey in broad daylight over land humans often visited, even if they didn't actually live there.

"I reckon," she said at length, "it's taken cover on a tor."

"That doesn't tell us much," Simon remarked, turning his head from one side to the other. "I can see five tors here."

"Yes," Pati agreed, "but the panther will be on one of those two." She pointed to the east.

"How do you know?" asked Simon.

"Because it won't go further out on to the moor. It will want to be within reach of the woodland, near the safety of cover. That's how panthers behave, so . . ."

She let her words die. Suddenly, the enormity of what they were doing came to her. They were on the moor, in touch with the mythical – but now, she knew, very real – panther. It was possible that they would be the first people to observe it closely and be able to prove, beyond any doubt, its existence.

Without speaking further, she reached into the side pocket of her rucksack and tugged out her camouflage forage cap. Very carefully, she wound her blonde hair up into a ball at the back of her head and, slipping the cap over it, pulled the peak down over her forehead.

She looked at Simon. She thought he seemed nervous.

"If you don't . . ." she began.

Simon shook his head. "No," he said, "I'm coming. I don't deny I'm scared. What if . . .?" He smiled a little sheepishly. "I suppose it's time to make my life an *it is*."

Pati punched him lightly on the shoulder and they set off, side by side, across the moor.

Chapter Eight
Stalking the Tor

THE TOR STOOD out starkly against the sky, two hundred metres ahead. A tall rock in the centre rose up like a square base from which the statue had been removed. Around its base was a tumble of large boulders, some of them half hidden by bushes.

71

"Panther country," Pati murmured decisively.

"How do we . . .?" Simon paused to choose the right words but none seemed to fit. "Go in."

"We split up," Pati said, keeping her voice low. "I'll come from the left, you from the right. Head for that tall bush above the smooth rock."

"What if it charges one of us?" Simon asked.

"It won't," Pati told him confidently although she was, herself, suddenly unsure of her facts. Lions and tigers charged when cornered. Of that, she was sure. Leopards and panthers, she thought, stood their ground or fled.

They moved a hundred metres apart. On Pati's signal, they started to cautiously approach the tor, half crouching to reduce their outline. Every now and then, a rabbit bolted in front of them or a bird rose from the scrub, calling shrilly as they approached its nest.

Under her breath, Pati cursed each one of them. Every patter of rabbits' paws on the earth, every flurry of wings in the air, every complaining, piping song of a worried hen with eggs or chicks in the heather, was an alarm signal to be heard and understood by their quarry.

As she edged forwards quietly, watching the tor ahead and taking great care not to place her foot on a sprig of dry heather, a twig or a loose stone, Pati remembered the day she saw her first leopard, the day on which she fell deeply, permanently in love with big cats.

One wet, miserable day on a fishing trip when the trout refused to rise, her father had taken her to a wildlife park. They had walked past cages of lemurs sitting hunched in the rain, enclosures of racoons hiding in wooden barrels, elephants standing motionless in their huge barn and wallabies huddling together under a bush like forlorn people in grey fur coats, waiting for a bus. Even the tortoises had drawn their heads and legs in.

Pati had been singularly unimpressed by all these animals. It was not until the end of their visit that they came upon a large cage in which some fallen tree trunks were arranged over a grassy paddock and an artificial rock cave. Several small bushes grew out of crevices above the entrance.

At first, Pati had seen nothing in the cage. Then, through the drizzle, she glimpsed a movement in the cave. Something big, immensely powerful and exquisitely graceful was moving in the darkness.

She strained her eyes to see what it was then studied the printed label on a board hanging from the bars of the cage. It read:

Panthera pardus – Leopard
Found throughout Africa, the Near and Middle East, Asia Minor (rare), India, South-east Asia, China, Korea, Manchuria: eradicated in some areas.

Lives in all types of habitat from rainforest to desert, lowland plain to mountain up to the snowline. Active by day and night. Secretive. Lies up in trees or in rocks. Feeds on any mammal, birds, reptiles, fish, insects; will eat fruit and carrion.

The leopard was in the open. It had not appeared slowly but seemed to have sprung from thin air – one moment it was not there, the next it was in full view. Drops of drizzle shone on its sleek, spotted coat. Its head was solid, as if carved of stone and covered tightly with fur. Its eyes were emotionless.

Pati had stood transfixed by it. Everything else in the world ceased to exist – the woman behind her with two small, complaining children; her father standing by her side; some monkeys chattering in another cage, alarmed by the appearance of the leopard – all vanished. It was as if she were alone in the world with this magnificent, awesome creature.

A twig snapped. Pati glanced at her feet. She was stepping, still half crouching, across a patch of mossy ground. There were no twigs anywhere near her hiking shoes.

There was a rustle in the bushes growing around the tumble of boulders at the foot of the tor, fifteen metres ahead. A dark shape slipped from beneath one hawthorn bush to vanish behind another. A stone the size of a tennis ball rolled a few metres down the slope and lodged in a clump of heather.

"Pati!" Simon called urgently. She could only just hear his voice. He was afraid to shout loudly in case he drew the creature's attention to himself.

She looked at him. He was pointing to the right-hand side of the tor. A dark shape, like the shadow of a dense and tiny cloud, slid under a rock and disappeared.

Pati stood up. There was no point in keeping low and silent now. The animal had gone. She eased her muscles. Her back and legs ached from crouching. Simon came across the heather towards her.

"I'm sorry," he said. "I think I must have alerted it."

"Don't worry, Si," Pati comforted him. "It knew we were coming. Let's see where it was lying up."

They scrambled over the boulders at the base of the tor. Some were the size of small cars, lying haphazardly against each other as if piled there by a giant's child who had tired of playing with its building bricks. In the nooks and crannies wild flowers, brambles, heather and wind-shaped bushes huddled, their branches growing to the shape of the stone against which they nestled.

"It came from under here," Simon announced as he clambered up the side of a smooth boulder. It was as steeply pitched as the roof of a house and, despite being dry and warm in the sun, just as slippery.

At the side of the boulder near the top, there was a dark, narrow entrance. Pati shrugged off her rucksack.

"You're not going in, are you?" Simon exclaimed, but Pati made no reply. She just slid her legs into the hole and started to wriggle her way behind the boulder.

It took a few moments for Pati's eyes to adjust to the gloom. The lair was like the cupboard under the stairs in her home, where the gas meter and the central-heating control box were. One wall was perpendicular, the other steeply sloping. The earth floor was bare and smooth with a slight depression in the centre. Clearly, this was a place the animal often visited.

Pati leaned slowly forward and pressed her hand to the depression. The earth was warm. It was then she sensed the delicate scent of panther lingering in the air, a mixture of sweetness and musk and blood.

"Pati!" Simon called urgently from outside. "Are you all right?"

"I'm OK," she replied.

"Come and see this," Simon answered, a distinct sense of relief in his voice.

Pati wormed her way back to the daylight. Simon was a little way off looking at the ground. She put on her rucksack and joined him.

"What've you got?" she asked.

On the ground, close to a clump of wiry grass, was a large dropping, not unlike a piece of fresh dog dung, but longer and thinner. Pati did not need to study it. She knew it did not belong to a fox, a dog or a badger. Matted into it was a tangle of wool.

"Where do you think it's gone?" Simon wondered.

"To the east," Pati decided, with immediate conviction. "It went round the right-hand side of the tor, so that can only mean it's headed for the woods on the edge of the moor. It'll feel safer there, in the cover of the trees where it's easier to hide."

"What do we do now?" Simon asked.

Pati looked him straight in the eye and said, "What do you think, Si? We follow it."

Chapter Nine
Deer Don't Climb Trees

IT TOOK THE better part of an hour for them to reach the edge of the woodland. They did not bother to try and track the panther across the moor. It would not have kept to paths but gone in a more or less straight line.

On the way, they met a man and his

wife walking their dogs – a golden retriever and a black collie-type mongrel. As they passed them by, saying hello, Pati wondered if the panther would, one day, take one of those dogs: dog was a leopard's favourite diet item and a panther was basically a leopard under another name. In India, she had read, leopards were actually called panthers.

Yet, no sooner had the thought come to her than she realized it would not happen. Where there were dogs there were humans and the panther would not risk a human confrontation. Besides, in all her press cuttings, she had not once read of a farmer missing his dog, only his sheep.

At the edge of the woods, they

stopped and rested for a quarter of an hour. Simon ate some chocolate. Pati chewed several of her high energy glucose tablets, which fizzed on her tongue. They drank to keep their body fluids up.

Then Simon went in one direction and Pati the other, working along the rim of the trees to find where the panther had entered the cover. The sun was well down before Pati found pug marks in the mud by a spring where the panther, hot from crossing the moor, had paused to drink.

"It's going to get dark in a couple of hours," Simon said.

"So?" Pati responded.

"So don't you think . . .?" Simon began.

Pati gave him a withering look and

said, "You've got to be yanking my chain, Si. You think I've come this far to give up?"

"We can come back at first light," Simon reasoned.

Pati knelt down and filled her canteen from the spring, where the water giggled and gurgled over a mossy stone.

"You can go back, Si," she said, "so long as you keep your mouth shut."

"That's rich!" Simon replied. "If I turn up without you, there'll be hell to pay."

Pati stood up, screwed the cap on her canteen and grinned. "You got an option, then, Si?" she asked.

"What about the Three Hs?" he said.

"Stuff the Three Hs!" Pati said sharply. "I'm not giving up."

Simon followed Pati's example and topped up his own canteen from the spring. He did not speak again until it was full and then, looking into the woodland, he said, "What if the Wisht Hound is really a Wisht *Cat*?"

"Don't be a prat, Si!" Pati scoffed. "It's a legend, not a scientific fact."

"All legends have a basis in truth," Simon defended himself.

"You'll be telling me the Devil really lives in Wistman's Wood next," Pati answered sarcastically, then she softened. "It's an old wives' tale, Si. Made up to scare naughty kids. Go to bed, eat your stewed cabbage or the Wisht Hound'll get you. That sort of thing. This is no satanic cat. It's a common or garden panther."

Simon smiled. Pati's confidence was catching.

"There's no common panthers in our garden," he said, his courage building.

"No," Pati replied. "They're all on my bedroom wall." She settled the straps of her rucksack over her shoulders. "Let's go."

With that, they stepped into the lengthening shadows of the trees.

Under the trees, it was a totally different world from the moor. The last rays of sunlight slanting in gave the woodland carpet of fallen leaves a deep bronze colour. In the beams, insects danced like flakes of gold dust. The shadows were stark and deep. The breeze that blew across the moorland was stilled here, the air calm and quiet.

The panther was easy to follow as, once in the trees, it had kept to a track made by deer. Its pug marks showed every so often in the dust. Furthermore, it had stopped at a tall, ancient oak to mark the trunk. The bark was still damp and pungent from its urine.

When the sun began to set, the woods took on a new character. The trees seemed to move closer to each other. The air cooled and started to smell faintly of damp leaves and toadstools.

Neither Pati nor Simon spoke. They didn't want to alarm their quarry and they were also both wrapped up in their own thoughts. Simon could not rid himself of a nagging doubt about Wisht Hounds. Pati concentrated on the ground ahead of her feet. Her every nerve was alert for any sign that they might be approaching the panther.

At last, Simon halted and whispered, "Can you smell it?"

Pati gently sniffed the air. She caught it too. It was the odour of putrefying meat. They looked around, but could see nothing in the deepening twilight.

Pati felt in the side pocket of her rucksack and took out her Mag-Lite torch. She twisted the head and a pencil-thin ray of bright halogen light shone across the woodland. Swinging it to and fro, she watched for the flash of eyes in the gloom. Nothing. Sure the panther was not near, she moved the light slowly across the ground. Still nothing.

Then it dawned on her. She pointed

the Mag-Lite into the trees. In the fork of a tall beech tree, something caught the light.

Not speaking, she stepped towards the tree. Simon followed in her footsteps.

Wedged into the fork was a dead roe deer. Blood from its nose streaked the smooth trunk of the tree.

"Deer don't climb trees," Simon muttered. "What's it doing up there?"

"I told you already, Si. Remember? Leopards and panthers instinctively take their kill into trees," Pati murmured, "to stop scavengers eating it." She switched the torch off. "That's a fresh kill," she went on. "It'll be back to feed. All we have to do is wait."

Chapter Ten
Panther

PATI FUMBLED IN her rucksack, removing the Canon. As she switched it on, the flash flicked up from the left-hand side of the camera body. She adjusted the picture mode to the night setting, moved the zoom lens halfway out, composed her shot and took several photos of the deer in quick succession. At each shutter release, the trees were momentarily illuminated by the brilliant flash, the film whirring on to the next frame.

"There," she said with a quiet satisfaction as she put the camera back in her rucksack, "that proves it doesn't just live off sheep."

Twenty metres away, a massive fallen tree lay on the ground. Pati and Simon settled themselves down against the trunk, pressing themselves against it to reduce their outline.

Night fell. The nocturnal woodland animals came to life. A little owl started calling. Tiny snufflings in the leaf litter announced the presence of the owl's prey, woodland mice and shrews. A fox started to cough a long way off. After an hour or so, a full moon rose, bathing the woodland in flat, white light.

The first they knew of the panther's arrival was the sound of it feeding on the roe deer. There was a soft tearing sound, followed by a lapping noise and the crack of a bone. Looking up, they could see the panther in full moonlight in the tree fork, lying half across the roe deer, pulling at the flesh on its shoulder.

Pati's heart thumped with excitement. At last! This was no leopard on her bedroom wall, no leopard in a cage with drizzling rain on its fur. This was a magnificent, wild, untamed creature, its coat glistening in the moonlight.

Simon, his anxiety gone, watched entranced as the panther fed with all the daintiness of a pet tabby. It did not snatch at the deer carcass like a lion or tiger might, but seemed almost to nibble at it.

After half an hour, the panther had had its fill. It moved to another branch in the tree and started to preen itself, cleaning its paws and washing its face and whiskers just like a domestic cat. It seemed to be utterly ignorant of its watchers.

Finally, it leapt to the ground in one bound but, instead of heading off the way it had come, it started in the direction of Pati and Simon. It walked with a purposeful step and did not halt until it was five metres from them, standing in a pool of moonlight. It was clear that the panther was fully aware of their presence and had probably been so throughout its feeding.

Pati and Simon held their breath, but their hearts were racing. Blood pounded through their veins. Every feature of the panther was clear, as if it was standing on a stage. Its rounded ears were up, its every whisker was clearly defined. Its black coat shone as richly as polished ebony. It looked straight at them, then without a sound, it turned and sauntered off, its long tail bounding slightly with each step.

"C'mon," Pati half whispered.

She and Simon got slowly to their feet and followed the panther. It made no attempt to flee, but kept up a steady ambling pace through the woods. After about half a mile, it halted and glanced over its shoulder as if to reassure itself that they were still there. Pati and Simon halted. As they watched, the panther disappeared. It might have been a ghost.

They approached the spot where it had been and found they were on the rim of a sheer cliff, beneath which the woodland stretched away across a narrow valley.

Pati lay down and peered over the edge. A few bushes sprouted here and there out of the cliff. About five metres down there was a ledge a metre wide. On it, in full moonlight, stood the panther. It looked up, its eyes meeting Pati's.

At that moment, some primitive message passed between them. It was a message older than mankind, from the dim past of creation when men were still wild and spoke the language of the animals. Yet Pati instinctively understood it. Something told her that the panther meant her no harm — and that it trusted her.

Simon joined her just as the animal stepped forward and vanished into the rock face.

"There's a cave down there," Pati whispered. "That's its den."

The moon shone brightly upon the cliff. The stones seemed to soak it up and give off a grey light of their own.

There was movement on the ledge. Pati sucked her breath in. In full view was a panther cub. She could tell it was a few weeks old because its eyes were open, but it was still unsteady on its legs. As she looked at it, it mewed a tiny, high-pitched little wail. It was joined by another.

"If there are cubs," Simon said, his voice barely audible, "there must be more than one adult . . ."

What made Pati look away from the cubs she could not say, but as she glanced at Simon, she happened to look over his shoulder.

Not ten metres away, at the edge of the cliff, stood a large black panther, its muscles filled out, the tip of its long tail flicking.

"The male," Pati whispered.

Simon turned his head, just a little too quickly. At the movement, the panther flattened its ears. The air filled with a growl so low-pitched they could barely hear it. It was like the distant, deep hum of angry bees. It made the very air vibrate.

"What next?" Simon whispered.

As if to answer him, the male lowered its belly slowly to the ground. Its mouth opened a centimetre or two to let out an ominous spitting hiss.

"It's going to spring," Pati murmured.

All the animal's muscles came into play at once. It was like watching a world-class athlete in a black fur coat moving off his blocks at the start of a hundred metre sprint. It leapt into the air towards them then, in mid-flight, it turned and was gone over the edge of the cliff.

Simon let out a huge sigh. It was only now he realized he had been holding his breath. Pati was speechless with awe. She wished it could all happen again, like an action replay.

"We should be getting back," Simon said quietly. "The male might return."

"I doubt it," Pati said. "It doesn't trust humans."

"What about our parents?" he added. "They'll be worried. My mother will —"

"I've got to photograph it," Pati declared.

"Do it then," Simon replied urgently, "and let's go."

"I can't," Pati answered.

"Why not? Your camera's got a flash," Simon said.

"I can't use the flash," Pati explained. "That would scare them, blind them. Besides," she went on, "we can't go back in the dark. We could get lost on the moor."

"The moonlight's bright," Simon reasoned.

"It doesn't light the way," Pati

retorted, "and it isn't clear, like daylight. You want to end up swallowed by a bog, your soul hunted for ever by the Wisht Hounds?"

Simon saw the logic. One wrong step off the path, one mistaken landmark and they could wind up in a quagmire. There was, he knew, no alternative but to stay until daylight.

For an hour, they watched the cubs with their mother. After she had suckled them, both cubs fell asleep between her paws whilst she dozed. Every time an owl hooted or a fox called, the panther woke instantly to survey the valley. Yet at no time did she pay her audience the least notice.

Eventually, Pati touched Simon's arm and nodded over her shoulder. As quietly as they could, they edged away from the rim of the cliff and spent the rest of the night curled up against the base of an oak tree, lying between the buttress roots, sleeping and keeping watch in turn, just in case.

The female panther accepted their presence, but the male might change his mind. Pati was only too conscious of the fact that a twitching tail on any cat meant it was annoyed and, on a male black panther, it could spell trouble.

Yet the male did not reappear and, as dawn broke, they crawled back to the cliff edge and looked over. In the early light, the cubs were playing with their mother's tail, batting it with their paws or tumbling over each other.

Pati waited until the first rays of

sunlight touched the cliff then, holding her camera out over the brink, she used up all her film. The panther did not take the slightest notice.

"Aren't they incredible?" she whispered, as the last film whirred and rewound.

Before Simon could reply, the panther suddenly sprang alert. The cubs scuttled out of sight into the cave.

"What's spooked her?" Simon muttered, but no sooner had he spoken than he heard it too. It was the far off *whup-whup-whup* of the rotors of a helicopter.

"The Three Hs!" Pati almost shouted. "Quick! We've got to get away from here. They mustn't find this place."

Snatching up their rucksacks, they ran

through the woods, keeping under the cover of the trees. They fled past the roe deer carcass in the beech tree, leapt over the fallen tree behind which they had hidden and headed for the edge of the woodland. Just before they reached the beginning of the moor, Pati grabbed Simon by the arm, almost causing him to stumble.

"We've got to have the same story," she said urgently. "We were on the moor, and we saw a deer, and we followed it into the woods, and night came on, and we got lost. We spent the night in a clearing by a fallen tree. We're cold and hungry, but otherwise OK. Got it?"

"Got it," Simon confirmed.

"Nothing else," Pati warned him. "No fancy lies, no other details or they'll catch us out. Act scared and glad to be saved."

Simon nodded. Side by side, they stepped out into the open. Across the moor, a quarter of a mile away, a line of men was moving steadily towards the woodland, some of them thrashing at the heather with sticks. Above them, a bright yellow Royal Navy Sea King Air-Sea Rescue helicopter hovered.

Pati ran forward, waving and blowing on her whistle. One of the men waved back. She recognized him as the leader of the platoon of slacking baboons from the Third Brigade. Others followed suit. The helicopter dipped its nose and headed for them, landing on a flat area of grass and rocks. The down-draught of its rotors thrashed the surrounding heather.

A man in a flying suit and helmet dropped down from the open doorway and ran towards them.

Within minutes, they were seated in the helicopter, swaddled in blankets. As the aircraft lifted off, Pati heard the pilot report over the radio, "Hotel Victor Quebec! We've found both of them. Tired and tuckered out, but none the worse for wear. Returning to rendezvous. Over!"

It took the Sea King less than ten minutes to fly back to the campsite. As it turned through 180 degrees to touch down, Pati could see their parents' caravans surrounded by police cars, several army lorries, two ambulances and a Volvo estate car with *Westcountry TV* painted across the roof. A camera crew was standing ready. Next to one of the ambulances, she could make out her own and Simon's parents.

Reaching out from under her blanket, she took hold of Simon's hand and dug her nails hard into his skin. At the same time, she gave him a meaningful stare. Simon winked back to say he understood.

The helicopter had hardly settled on the ground before Pati's mother was at its side. She grabbed her daughter and hugged her so tightly Pati could hardly breathe.

"Oh, Pati!" she cried, kissing her as tears rolled down her face. "You're safe! You're safe, darling! We were so worried."

Simon's mother similarly hugged him

and said, "Are you all right, Simon? We were afraid . . ."

When the ambulance men and a doctor had checked them over and pronounced them unharmed, Pati and Simon were given mugs of hot chocolate. As they sat sipping their drinks, a television reporter came over, the cameraman switched on his lights and they were interviewed.

The reporter asked them all the predictable questions – how did they get lost, how had they spent the night, how were they feeling now? Pati and Simon stuck to their story.

Finally, the reporter came to the end of his interview and asked, "Weren't you afraid of meeting the Black Panther of the Moors?"

Simon gave Pati a sideways glance.

"No," Pati answered quite firmly. "We were never afraid of the panther."

Chapter Eleven
Yes!

THE SOUNDS OF lunch break could just be heard through the boarded, blacked-out window of the St Audrey's Comprehensive School photographic club darkroom, next door to Lab Two in the Science Block. Shouts arose from the playground where at least forty boys were playing one game of football.

From immediately below came muffled laughter and the faint reek of coffee and cigarette smoke. The darkroom was directly above the staffroom.

Pati fumbled for the light switch and flicked it on. The darkroom filled with a warm, red glow from the safety lamp mounted on the wall. She pressed a button on the developing tank. The sealed, light-proof drum containing her first print whirred this way and that, driven by an electric motor, spreading the developer over the sheet of exposed photographic paper held inside it.

At exactly the right moment dictated by the second hand on the wall-mounted clock, she tipped the drum up and drained the developer out through the nozzle. She ran warm water through it to clean the paper then added the fixer. Once more she watched the jerking second hand. Then she rinsed the drum through eight times with clean water.

As she unscrewed the drum lid, her hands shook slightly. This was the moment of truth. With a pair of plastic tweezers, she removed the photograph and spread it on the steel sheet by the sink. Then, with a window cleaner's rubber-bladed squeegee bar, she removed the excess water.

Hardly daring to look at the photograph, she moved the steel sheet to the other end of the workbench and started to wave a small hairdryer over it.

At first, the colours were hazy and slightly tinged with red.

Pati was not unduly perturbed. Colour prints were always like this. She was far more afraid that she might have got the exposure wrong in the first place, or that the camera had not focused accurately, or that the film was somehow faulty.

As the photograph dried, the reddish tint vanished and the colours sharpened. It was like seeing a faint mist lift from the image – like seeing, Pati thought, the early morning fog rising off the moors.

Finally, when the photograph was thoroughly dry, she picked it up, opened the darkroom door and walked across to the windows of the laboratory.

Below in the playground, the football game was in an enforced half-time. A fight had broken out over a disputed goal or tackle and the duty teacher had arrived on the scene. Play was suspended while he read the riot act to the squabbling players. Across the other side of the cricket pitch and running track, traffic was speeding along the bypass close to the school boundary fence.

Pati looked down at the photograph that she was holding carefully in both hands, as if it were a valuable book.

For a long moment, she studied it then, looking out across the playground, she uttered just one triumphant word.

"Yes!"

That afternoon, Pati had Geography followed by English, then French in the last double period. Simon was out of school, attending special cricket coaching classes at the county cricket club ground. All through her lessons, she sat hardly able to concentrate. When the bell went at four o'clock, she was first out of the school gate.

Simon had not returned to school from his coaching session. He had gone straight into town to where he and Pati had agreed to meet. By half-past four, he was sitting on the bench outside McDonald's in the High Street, eating chips from a cardboard container. Next to him on the bench was a cardboard cup of shake.

He looked at his watch for the third time in as many minutes. Pati was late. She should have met him at a quarter past. He began to worry that something had gone wrong, although he could not imagine what it was.

"Hi, Si!"

He turned. Pati was standing behind him. She leaned over the bench and picked up his shake.

"What is it?" she asked.

"Vanilla," Simon replied and he tried to snatch the cup away. Pati jerked backwards out of reach, sucking hard on the straw until there was a hollow slurping.

"You've drunk it all!" Simon complained.

Pati grinned and came round the bench. She handed him the empty cup and sat down. Silently, she looked at the passing traffic circling the roundabout outside Barclays Bank and Marks & Spencer.

"Well," Simon finally inquired, "did you do them?" He sucked hopefully on the straw, but all he got was froth.

Pati opened her school sports bag and removed from it a blue plastic wallet. On the cover was printed a coloured picture of a pretty woman in a bikini holding a gaudy beach ball. Above the picture were the words 'KwikSnaps Kwality 24-Hour Service'.

"You didn't take them into a shop, did you?" Simon asked in disbelief. "I thought we were keeping it secret . . ."

"I'm not as green as I'm cabbage-looking," Pati retorted sharply. "That's just to keep them in."

"So?" Simon said impatiently, throwing the empty cup into a litter bin by the bench. "What have you got?"

Slowly, Pati opened the wallet and handed it to Simon. In the transparent first page was a ten by fifteen centimetre photograph. In it, the panther was looking straight into the camera, straight into Simon's eyes as if it was searching for his soul.

"Unbelievable!" Simon whispered, almost reverently.

"That," Pati announced in a quiet but jubilant tone, "is my panther."

Music on the Bamboo Radio

Martin Booth

1941. The Imperial Japanese Army invades Hong Kong. All Europeans are rounded up and imprisoned. But one boy slips the net . . .

Nicholas Holford, disguised as a Chinese, soon finds himself involved with the Communist guerrillas and is given a perilous mission – to smuggle information to British troops in prisoner-of-war camps. It's called 'playing music on the bamboo radio', and discovery means torture and certain death . . .

'A thrilling reconstruction . . . of partly forgotten history and a powerfully appropriate reminder of the realities of enemy occupation . . . an impressively readable book' – *The Times*

'Superbly told' – *Sunday Telegraph*

READ MORE IN PUFFIN

For children of all ages, Puffin represents quality and variety – the very best in publishing today around the world.

For complete information about books available from Puffin – and Penguin – and how to order them, contact us at the appropriate address below. Please note that for copyright reasons the selection of books varies from country to country.

On the worldwide web: www.penguin.co.uk

In the United Kingdom: Please write to *Dept. EP, Penguin Books Ltd, Bath Road, Harmondsworth, West Drayton, Middlesex UB7 0DA*

In the United States: Please write to *Penguin Putnam inc., P.O. Box 12289, Dept B, Newark, New Jersey 07101-5289* or call 1-800-788-6262.

In Canada: Please write to *Penguin Books Canada Ltd, 10 Alcorn Avenue, Suite 300, Toronto, Ontario M4V 3B2*

In Australia: Please write to *Penguin Books Australia Ltd, P.O. Box 257, Ringwood, Victoria 3134*

In New Zealand: Please write to *Penguin Books (NZ) Ltd, Private Bag 102902, North Shore Mail Centre, Auckland 10*

In India: Please write to *Penguin Books India Pvt Ltd, 11 Panscheel Shopping Centre, Panscheel Park, New Delhi 110 017*

In the Netherlands: Please write to *Penguin Books Netherlands bv, Postbus 3507, NL-1001 AH Amsterdam*

In Germany: Please write to *Penguin Books Deutschland GmbH, Metzlerstrasse 26, 60594 Frankfurt am Main*

In Spain: Please write to *Penguin Books S. A., Bravo Murillo 19, 1° B, 28015 Madrid*

In Italy: Please write to *Penguin Italia s.r.l., Via Felice Casati 20, I-20124 Milano*

In France: Please write to *Penguin France S. A., 17 rue Lejeune, F-31000 Toulouse*

In Japan: Please write to *Penguin Books Japan, Ishikiribashi Building, 2-5-4, Suido, Bunkyo-ku, Tokyo 112*

In South Africa: Please write to *Longman Penguin Southern Africa (Pty) Ltd, Private Bag X08, Bertsham 2013*